Martha Dreams of Dino saurs

By Christy Watson

Martha Dreams of Dinosaurs
By Christy Watson

Cover art by: Christy Watson
Story & Illustration by: Christy Watson
Design by: Craig Watson

First Edition: 2018

Revision 2_vIS

ISBN-13: 978-1-7327606-0-8

Yellow Sun Books
USA

The Illustrations in this book were done with markers and pen.

For more information: *YellowSunBooks.com* or *yellowsunbooks@gmail.com*

Yellow Sun Books

To
Grayson
Dinosaur Technical Advisor, my buddy, and my inspiration,

and

Joshua
My whispered encourager, who is probably riding a dinosaur right now.

I would also like to thank my amazing family and friends who encouraged me, listened to my ideas and my fears, and supported me not only with this book but throughout my life, especially the last of the Schneider matriarchy: my mom, my sisters, my aunts and my cousins, including the honorary ones. Special thanks to: my husband Craig Watson, who supports me and my dreams, who is an incredibly gifted writer and graphic designer, and without whom this book may not have happened; Johnny Marszalkowski, who gave me not only encouragement and technical help but a deadline and launch, too; Kate Burden Kent, whose effervescence and positivity is contagious; Cyndi Hall, for editing this book and double checking every little thing; and all my nieces and nephews, who give me inspiration and an audience for which to write.

Martha is a ladybug.

That is to say, a lady ladybug.

Hello

She lives in a tiny house in a big tree, in a field very much like fields near where you live.

Her home is very little because Martha is very little.

During the day, Martha does small things like other ladybugs.

She has a small bath in a couple of drops of rainwater caught in a little bucket.

She makes funny little hairdos with the tiny soap bubbles.

She wears the absolutely teeniest, tiniest, littlest mini pink bow on one of her antennae.

She does it because she likes to have a little fun.

In the afternoon, Martha makes tea in her little kettle and bakes delicious tiny cakes in her little oven.

She likes cakes because she has an itsy-bitsy sweet tooth.

Sometimes Martha has a lovely little chat with her little friend Stewart.

They sit on small sticks and talk about how wonderful it is to be so little, in small voices.

In the evening, she wears her tiny red glasses and reads her tiny books in her small comfy chair.

You see, everything about Martha is small.

However...

...at night, when Martha goes to sleep in her little bed, tucked under her small blankets, cuddled up with her little head on her little pillow, Martha dreams of **BIG THINGS.**

Martha Dreams of Dino saurs!

She dreams of large Velociraptors.

The Velociraptors are smaller than most dinosaurs, but much bigger than Martha.

They play a great big game of leapfrog with each other, taking big jumps high into the air.

They try to touch the large clouds floating overhead.

Martha dreams she has a lovely big chat with her large Stegosaurus friend.

They sit on a huge tree branch and talk about how wonderful it is to be so big, in loud voices.

Martha dreams she soars with the massive Pterosaur against a ginormous orange sky.

Their long wings spread out
and glide on the big wind, circling
the great, huge, gigantic volcano
very far below.

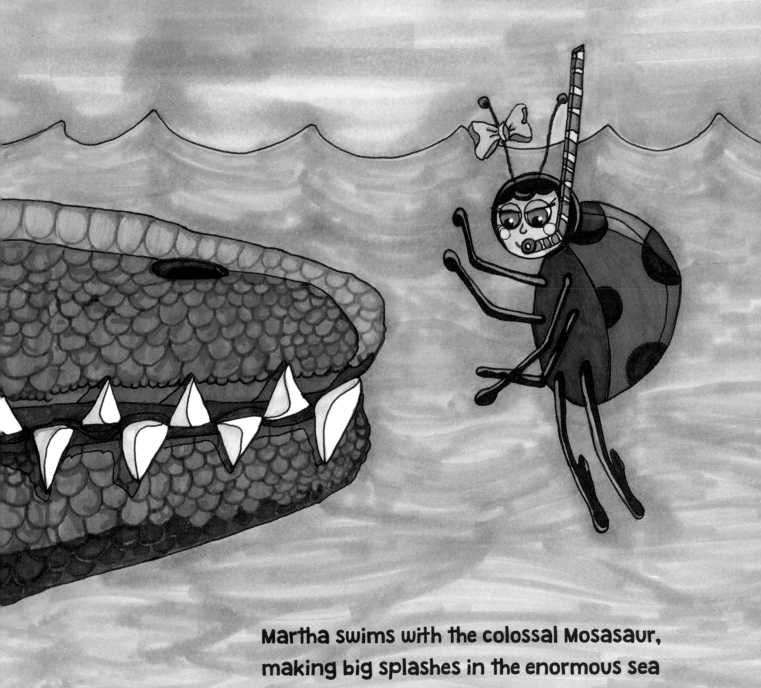

Martha swims with the colossal Mosasaur, making big splashes in the enormous sea of blues and greens.

Back on land, Martha loudly stomps across a vast dirt field with a giant Tyrannosaurus Rex.

They leave big footprints in the mud.

They open their big mouths, full of big teeth, and a big tongue, and let out a colossal roar!

...and finds herself in her little bed, tucked under her little blankets, cuddled up with her little head on her little pillow.

Martha gets up, stretches her tiny legs, and smiles.

She loves being small, and she loves dreaming big.

Martha knows that even little lady ladybugs, and small creatures everywhere, can have

Big, huge, giant, colossal

Dreams.

The End.

CPSIA information can be obtained
at www.ICGtesting.com
Printed in the USA
LVIC051623260319
611894LV00019B/474